The Muppet Babies live in a nursery
in a house on a street that is a lot like yours.
But they can travel anywhere anytime using a special power—
the power of the imagination.
Can you imagine what it would be like to go with them?
Join the Muppet Babies on this adventure and find out.

Weekly Reader Presents

Good Knight, Sir Kermit

By Michaela Muntean • Illustrated by Sue Venning

Muppet Press • New York

Weekly Reader Books offers several exciting
card and activity programs. For information,
write to WEEKLY READER BOOKS, P.O. Box 16636,
Columbus, Ohio 43216.

This book is a presentation of
Weekly Reader Books.

Weekly Reader Books offers book clubs for children
from preschool through high school.

For further information write to:
Weekly Reader Books
4343 Equity Drive
Columbus, Ohio 43228

Weekly Reader is a trademark of Field Publications.

Printed in the United States of America

It was a summer evening, the kind when bedtime
arrives before it is dark.

"I don't like having to go to bed while it's still
light outside," Kermit sighed. "We could be playing
in the park."

"Try playing with your toes," Gonzo suggested. "That always makes me sleepy."

"Sleep is a waste of time," Kermit decided. "When I grow up, I'm going to stay up as late as I want and do all kinds of exciting things. I may *never* go to sleep!" Then he reached out and took a big storybook from the nursery bookshelf.

The storybook was filled with pictures of knights in shining armor and fire-breathing dragons and huge castles surrounded by moats.

"I bet the babies who lived back then had exciting lives," said Kermit. "They probably stayed up all night fighting dragons and having fun."

Kermit studied a picture of a grey stone castle. "It must have been great to live in a place like this," he thought. "You would never run out of rooms to explore. I wonder what's behind the castle. I wish I could see…"

Suddenly, Kermit was no longer looking at a picture.
He was peeking around the corner of a *real* castle—
a castle just like the one in his storybook.

Now he could see that behind the castle was a beautiful garden. In the middle of the garden was a pond filled with lily pads, and on one of the lily pads, a frog—who was just about his own size—lay sleeping.

"That frog looks familiar," Kermit thought, and he jumped into the pond to have a better look.

As Kermit neared the lily pad, the sleeping frog woke with a start. "Who goes there?" he cried. Then he saw Kermit and shrugged his shoulders. "Never mind," he mumbled sleepily. "I thought you were the dragon."

"You must have been dreaming," Kermit laughed.
"Dragons aren't real. They're only in storybooks."
    "Of course they're real," the other frog answered.
"They're just as real as I am, and I am Sir Dance-a-lot,
Knight of the Pond Table!"

"My name is Kermit," said Kermit, "but I'm not a knight. I'm just plain old Kermit."

"You're lucky," Sir Dance-a-lot sighed, "because if you were me, you would have to fight the dragon today."

"Are you afraid?" Kermit asked.

"No, I'm exhausted," Dance-a-lot moaned. "I stayed up all night dancing. Dancing is my favorite thing to do. But if I had been a good knight, I would have gotten a good night's sleep! Now I'm really in trouble."

Sir Dance-a-lot then told Kermit his sad tale. A fire-breathing dragon had charged into the nearby town, demanding to marry the lovely Princess Pigdowlyn. Dance-a-lot was in love with Pigdowlyn and had challenged the dragon to a duel. Whoever could fight the longest would win the beautiful princess. Whoever got tired and stopped would lose.

"But I've had so little sleep," wailed Dance-a-lot, "I can barely stand up, let alone fight."

Kermit felt terribly sorry for the exhausted knight and wanted to help. "What if I fight the dragon for you?" he suggested. "I'm wide awake."

"Oh, thank you!" said the grateful knight, shaking Kermit's hand. "My armor and horse are behind that big rock. Be sure to wake me up when it's over. And good luck!"

Kermit was so excited, he could hardly put on the armor. He clinked and clanked around a bit, but he finally got it right and climbed on the horse. Then he headed toward town.

Kermit arrived to find a large crowd gathered to watch the duel. He rode closer until he had a good view of the dragon's huge golden eyes and glistening golden-green scales. The dragon looked strong, as though he could fight for a long, long time.

"Dance-a-lot, my hero!" Princess Pigdowlyn was calling. "You must save me from this monster. He has been running around breathing fire and smoke all night, waiting for you."

"So the dragon has been up all night, too, has he?" murmured Kermit as he took his position in front of the huge monster. "That gives me an idea."

When the duel began, Kermit tried to remember every lullabye he had ever heard. He sang them to the dragon one by one. He sang "Rock-a-bye Dragon." He sang "Go to Sleep Little Dragon" and "Dream Sweet Dragon Dreams."

Slowly, the dragon's eyes began to close. He sank to his knees, then stretched out on the ground. Soon he was sound asleep.

"Hip Hurrah! Long live Sir Dance-a-lot!" cheered the crowd. They cheered softly so as not to wake the dragon.

"My hero!" sighed Princess Pigdowlyn. "You have conquered the dragon, and now we can be married." She leaned over to give Kermit a kiss.

"Oh, no!" thought Kermit. "This is going too far. Fighting dragons is one thing, but marrying a princess is another. I'd better get the real Sir Dance-a-lot."

"Excuse me, Your Royal Pigginess," Kermit said with a bow. "I fear I have forgotten something very important. I will return shortly."

Kermit rode to the garden as quickly as he could. The real frog knight was waking up just as he arrived.

"Hurry," said Kermit as he took off the armor and handed it to Dance-a-lot. "Put yourself into this tin suit. We've got to get you back so you can marry the princess."

As they galloped along, Kermit told Dance-a-lot everything that had happened. "And if I were really you," Kermit said at the end of his story, "I would find something useful for that dragon to do when he wakes up."

The preparations for the wedding feast were well under way when the dragon finally awakened. He was very disappointed to find out that he had lost both the duel and the princess.

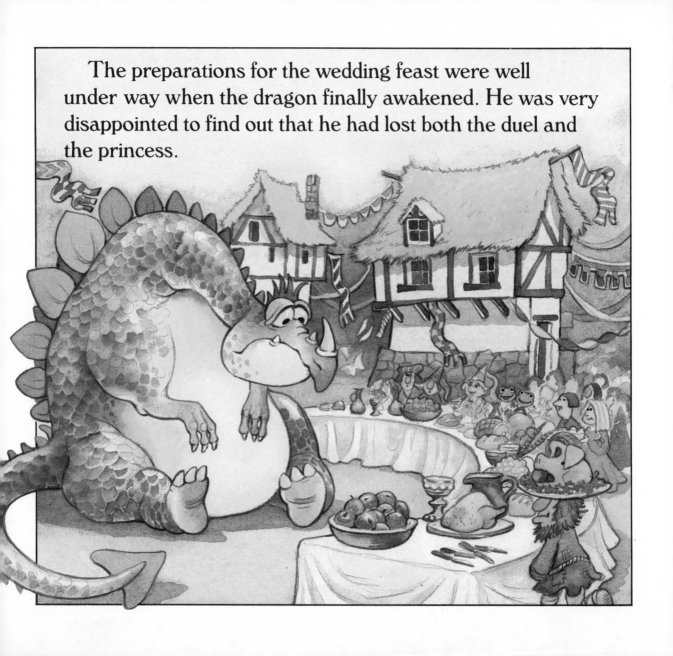

"Sigh, sigh, sigh," breathed the dragon, and every time he sighed, a flame flickered out of his mouth.

"Look!" exclaimed Princess Pigdowlyn in amazement. "He's roasting all the marshmallows with his fiery breath."

Kermit and Dance-a-lot stared at the dragon and then at each other. They both had the same idea.

"How would you like a job as Royal Chef?" Sir Dance-a-lot asked the dragon. The dragon was delighted because he loved to cook. His first job, of course, was to finish the wedding feast. He stewed tomatoes for tomato soup, he grilled the grilled cheese sandwiches, and he melted chocolate for hot fudge sundaes à la dragon.

Kermit had a wonderful time at the wedding, but after his busy day, he was finally beginning to feel sleepy.

Dance-a-lot thanked Kermit for everything he had done. Then he asked him to kneel. Drawing his sword, Dance-a-lot said, "For your bravery and untiring devotion, I now dub thee Sir Kermit, Knight of the Pond Table."

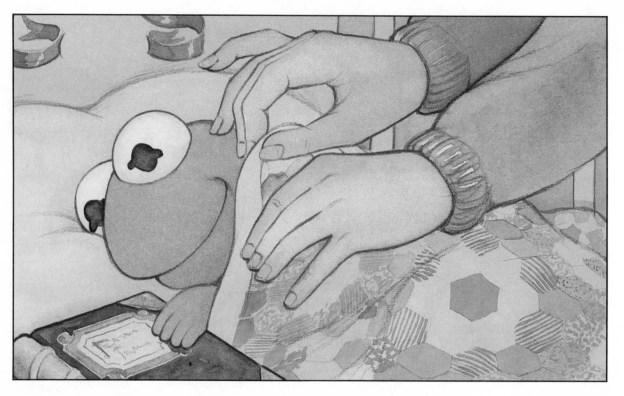

Kermit looked up, but he did not see Sir Dance-a-lot.
Instead he saw Nanny, who was tucking him into his own
little crib.

"Good night, Kermit," she said.

"Yes, Nanny," Kermit murmured sleepily. "I guess I am
a good knight. And like all good knights, I'm ready for a
good night's sleep."